ATTACK
ON THE
OVERWORLD

AN UNOFFICIAL OVERWORLD ADVENTURE, BOOK TWO

ATTACK
ON THE
OVERWORLD

DANICA DAVIDSON

Sky Pony Press
New York

Sky Pony Press books may be purchased in bulk at special discounts for
sales promotion, corporate gifts, fund-raising, or educational purposes.
Special editions can also be created to specifications. For details, contact
the Special Sales Department, Sky Pony Press, 307 West 36th Street,
11th Floor, New York, NY 10018 or info@skyhorsepublishing.com.

Sky Pony® is a registered trademark of Skyhorse Publishing, Inc.®, a
Delaware corporation.

Visit our website at www.skyponypress.com.

10 9 8 7 6 5 4 3 2 1

Library of Congress Cataloging-in-Publication Data is available on file.

Cover design by Brian Peterson
Cover artwork by Lordwhitebear

Print ISBN: 978-1-5107-0276-9
Ebook ISBN: 978-1-5107-0277-6

Printed in Canada

ATTACK
ON THE
OVERWORLD

CHAPTER 1

"I WANT TO SHOW YOU SOMETHING REALLY SCARY," Maison said.

My heart started pounding immediately. We were sitting in her room—in her world—and I knew from her voice it had to be something really bad. I'd only known Maison for a couple of months, but it had been enough time for us to become best friends, and for me to learn Maison didn't scare easily.

Maison and I were from two different worlds. My home was in the Overworld, where I lived with my dad, Steve, and our cat, Ossie. I was named Stevie after my dad, but sometimes it felt as if we couldn't be more different. My dad was always in-charge and knew about everything, and it felt like I was always messing up in one way or another. It wasn't all that long ago I was so caught up in trying to make a tree house that I wasn't paying attention to my safety and I was attacked by a creeper and some zombies.

I was getting better at building and fighting, though sometimes I still struggled in those areas. Dad taught me

1

how to plant, and farm, and mine for emeralds, and fight off monsters, which were also known as mobs. This was our life.

Maison lived in . . . well, I don't know what this world was named. But things came in all different shapes, and her mom worked as an architect instead of a farmer or miner, and they traded green stuff known as "money" at stores instead of making their own things. Maison went to a place each day called school; instead of going to school, I mainly worked with Dad and learned from life experiences.

Our worlds also had different things to do for fun. I liked to ride on pigs, using carrots to make them run. Maison liked to play baseball, a game she was trying to teach me. But I just can't get the hang of using sticks to hit balls instead of using sticks to build other things, like swords.

I didn't know her world even *existed* until I found a portal out to it. She'd known about my world, but she thought it was all a make-believe place on a game called *Minecraft*. She'd made a special portal in the Overworld while playing the game, and when I was attacked by a giant spider, I'd had no choice but to jump through the strange portal. I'd stepped out of her computer screen and into her world, changing both our lives forever.

It had all been pretty amazing at first, finding this world with different shapes and different people. They even had things on their hands called fingers, which I secretly thought looked like little squid tentacles. Don't tell Maison I said that, because she got offended the last time I mentioned it.

But things got scary fast, because the portal allowed zombies, giant spiders and a creeper to get out as well. They attacked the school. Maison and I fought them back, and then built a protective house around the portal in the Overworld so the mobs couldn't get to Maison's world again. Even though Maison had never seen real zombies or giant spiders before, she hadn't panicked. She'd stepped right up to the battle, and together, we saved the school.

So I knew Maison was pretty brave. That meant that if she was scared about something, I was scared about something.

"What is it?" I asked her now.

"Here," she said. "It'd just be easier to show you."

She took me to her computer, which was just sitting there looking like any other computer in her world. We were the only ones who knew it was also a portal to the Overworld.

"Did you open another portal?" I wondered. Maybe she'd accidentally opened a portal to the Nether, which was a pretty scary place. Or maybe she'd found an even scarier world neither one of us knew about! Anything was possible.

"No, nothing like that," she said, her squid tentacles . . . er, I mean *fingers* . . . typing quickly. The screen changed, and I knew this was some kind of a website she was showing me. Besides teaching me a lot of new words, Maison had also told me about things she had in her world, like *websites*.

In the Overworld, we had things like walking skeletons and Endermen and baby zombies that rode on chickens. In Maison's world, there wasn't anything like that, but they did have computers, where you could find out anything with a few clicks of a button. You could even watch a "video" (another word I'd learned from Maison) that showed you real things that had happened, even *after* they had happened.

There was a video on top of this webpage. A single page on a website was called a webpage, which I guess made sense. When the video started to play, it showed a grown woman holding a microphone and talking to Maison, who looked a little awkward.

"Welcome back to our nightly news program," the woman was saying. "I'm here interviewing Maison, an eleven-year-old local hero who saved her middle school. Now, Maison, has it been solved why all those zombies and spiders attacked your school?"

"Um, no," Maison said, not wanting to admit what was really going on. Maison and I had agreed it would be safer for both our worlds if other people didn't know about the computer portal.

"No one has ever seen anything like it," the woman said. "An unprotected middle school full of children suddenly under the onslaught of vicious monsters wanting nothing more than your utter destruction."

"She's kind of dramatic-sounding," I whispered now.

"Shhh," Maison whispered back to me.

"Yet, in the midst of your panic, you took charge," the woman on the video continued. "How did you find the courage?"

"Sometimes life doesn't really give you a choice," Maison said in the video. "Sometimes you just have to do the right thing."

"Profound words from someone so young!" the woman gushed in response. "There was also a young boy who was there, helping you. Witnesses said he looked like a *Minecraft* character, and they said that you introduced him earlier as your cousin, Stevie. Some other witnesses reported that you said in the auditorium that he really wasn't your cousin, but someone who came out of *Minecraft*. Which, of course, is impossible. And when I talked to your mother, Maison, she said you don't have a cousin named Stevie. Can you clear this up for us?"

Now Maison really looked uncomfortable in the video. I felt bad for her. "Well, I think there was just some misunderstanding," she said to the woman. "Things were pretty crazy with the school under attack and all that, and sometimes people get their details mixed up when big, stressful things happen."

The interview went on for a couple more minutes, with the woman insisting over and over that Maison was a hero and Maison looking like she was enjoying this and embarrassed by it at the same time. Then the video ended.

"So what's so scary about that?" I asked after a moment.

"Well, being on camera was kind of scary," Maison said. "It was a live interview, which means it was playing on TV right when I was talking to her. But that's not what I want to show you. Look."

She scrolled down lower on the page and my eyes widened.

"It's called a message board," Maison was explaining. "Someone put the video on top of the message board for people to talk about. Look at what they wrote."

But I was already reading it.

DestinyIsChoice123: Maison thinks she's so hot. She makes me sick. She's no hero. She's not even that good at baseball.

TheVampireDragon555: Just a misunderstanding?! Wow, that Maison's stupid. Can't believe that stupid newscaster bought it, too. They're both stupid.

Frankie_the_Squidking: You guys shouldn't be saying bad things about Maison. I'm a sixth grader at her school and I know her personally. She's the real deal. She helped my friends Jeremy, Dalton, Tobias and me fight off the zombies. We couldn't have done that without her.

TheVampireDragon555: @Frankie_the_Squidking: You're stupid. I know Maison's hiding something, and I'm going to prove it. In fact, I hope she's reading this right now. Hey, MAISON! We're coming for you. We know where you live.

DestinyIsChoice123: She's not going to think she's hot stuff for much longer, is she?

TheVampireDragon555: When we're through with her, she's going to regret ever getting out of bed in the morning. Hear that, Maison? Tick-tock, count the clock: we'll see you soon.

I scratched my head. "I'm confused. Why do they have names like DestinyIsChoice123 or TheVampire-Dragon555?"

"Those aren't their real names," Maison said. "They're made-up names, so they can post anonymously. That means you don't know who they really are."

"So they could be anybody typing this anywhere in your world?" I asked.

"Well, yeah," she said. "But they said they know where I live!"

"Don't you want people to know where you live?" I asked. "Everyone around us knows where my dad and I live. That's how you get friends."

Well, that might have been a little much on my part. The truth was, Maison really was my only good friend. Sometimes I played with the other kids in the village when Dad and I went to visit, but I never really felt welcomed by them.

Maison sounded pretty upset now. "No, Stevie," she said. "Don't you get it? Two people are threatening me online!"

"Well . . . have they shown up?" I asked.

"No," she said. "But I'm scared they're going to."

"I don't get it," I said. "What's so scary about this?"

Then I thought I understood. "One of them really *is* a dragon!" I exclaimed, thinking of the Ender Dragon. Of course I'd never seen the Ender Dragon, but Dad had told me tons of stories. "So this message board is proof that a dragon got out of the portal and is trying to contact you!"

I could see why Maison would be scared of that. *I* was scared of that. I'd never dealt with a dragon before. "What's a Vampire?" I asked, because that part was still confusing me. "Is that some kind of mob in your world?"

I really was trying to be helpful, but Maison was looking at me as if I couldn't be more clueless, and it seemed to bother her. Even after knowing each other for a couple months, sometimes we still got mixed up on something that was normal in one of our worlds but not in the other.

For instance, she couldn't understand why I loved mushroom soup so much—she said it tasted nasty and a cheeseburger was better. And I couldn't understand why so many people in her world were scared of spiders. The spiders they had were so tiny! I'd fought against giant spiders from the Overworld, so the little spiders in Maison's world made me want to laugh.

"It's not a dragon," she said. "And vampires are monsters that suck blood in old stories. But stuff like that isn't real. It's a person threatening me."

"People aren't dangerous like dragons or . . . uh, vampires," I said. "What's a person going to do?" People couldn't turn you into a zombie. They weren't going to suck your blood, either, like that vampire mob from the stories in her world.

"It's called 'cyberbullying,'" Maison said. "It's like bullying, but it's done online. My mom gave me a talk about cyberbullying awhile ago, and she told me cyberbullies were just sad kids trying to get a rise out of me. She said I should ignore them. I haven't told her about this, but now I'm starting to wonder if I should."

"I don't think it's anything to worry about," I said.

We'd run into some tough kids at Maison's middle school. They were mean, but they never physically hurt us or anything. And after Maison saved their lives during the mob attack, they'd stopped being bullies. Plus, it seemed to me those bullies were much more threatening than anyone typing on a computer.

"Zombies, giant spiders . . . those are scary," I went on. "And you showed you could take care of them."

"It's not just this message board, though," Maison said. "Any time there's an article about me, I find them writing comments underneath. DestinyIsChoice123 and TheVampireDragon555. They're following me online. And there's something else. Did you see how DestinyIsChoice123 said that I wasn't that good at baseball?"

"You're great at baseball," I said.

"That's not the thing," Maison said. "How do they know I even play baseball? It doesn't say that in any of the news reports. It's not information I have online. If they know I play baseball . . . they must have seen me play at the school or at the park. I think they really do know where I live."

I didn't have an answer to that. But I said, "I'm sure there's nothing to worry about. How about we go to our tree house in the Overworld and build some things?"

CHAPTER 2

BUILDING WAS MY WAY OF TRYING TO CHEER MAISON up. Maison was an amazing builder, and she always liked making something. Since my original tree house had been destroyed by a creeper, she and I had built a new one that was even better. We had a balcony and everything. We'd even made all the furniture inside so it felt homey, though we just used it as a place to hang out, not to live.

Now we sat up in the tree house, enjoying the sunshine, making ourselves stone swords. A stone sword took one stick and two pieces of cobblestone, and we used our newly-created crafting table to do the work.

Making the swords distracted Maison a little, but not that much. There was another reason why I wanted to hang out in the tree house and make swords: it kept me from studying my potions.

After the mob attack on Maison's school, Dad decided he needed to ramp up my studying. He said that since I was eleven now, it was time I really knew how to take care of myself if danger reared its head. He'd taught me how to build different things and how to sword fight, but I didn't know potions so well.

Why? Because potions were *boring*.

Maybe they would have been fun if I got to make them, but all Dad wanted me to do was memorize the ingredients that went into each potion. Dad was constantly quizzing me at the breakfast table or at the dinner table about different potions.

"Stevie," he'd say. "How do you make a Potion of Weakness? How do you make a Potion of Swiftness?"

But the more I tried to memorize them, the more they all got mixed up in my head. And that would just get Dad frustrated, which made me more frustrated. I really was trying to memorize them. Really.

"I think making potions sounds fun," Maison said now, after I told her about Dad's potion tirade. "I make potions sometimes when I play *Minecraft*."

"Yeah, you get to *make* them," I said. "But all I get to do is list off what's in them. And we could make a whole bunch of potions if he let me, because my dad has a ton of supplies in his shed."

That was Dad for you: he had to be ready for everything. He'd made his special diamond sword when he was only twelve, and that was just the beginning for what was to come. Now Dad had built multiple houses, kept a shed full of supplies, and had recorded every potion known in the Overworld into a series of books he kept in the den. It was exhausting trying to follow in Dad's footsteps. Around here, he was known as "The Steve" because of all his accomplishments.

"Mmm," Maison said absentmindedly. I could tell her mind was still on the "cyberbullies."

I glanced over at her. It was funny how we both looked so similar and so different. We both had black hair and brown, olive-toned skin, but while I was a blocky shape like the other people in the Overworld, Maison had all different proportions. Her face was oval like an emerald, her hair was wispy like spiderwebs in the mines and—I'd only learned this recently—she also had another pair of smaller squid tentacles on her feet. But instead of calling them feet-fingers, they were called toes. I discovered them when she wore a pair of "sandals," and she'd told me to quit staring.

"So, I don't get it," I said. "In your world, you have computers. With them, you can find any book, learn about any topic, and unearth any kind of knowledge. In the Overworld, we don't have anything like that. So with all those options you have, why do people just use it to be mean to others?"

Maison shrugged. "My mom said it's because some people feel small. They feel safer attacking a person behind a computer. Besides, people use computers for other things, too."

"Like what?" I asked.

"Well," Maison said, "we look at videos of cute animals, take surveys on which Disney character we'd be, and upload pictures of our breakfast."

I just stared at her. Sometimes her world made no sense at all.

"Oh," she said, "we also like to upload videos of the buildings we make in *Minecraft*."

I lightened up. "That sounds fun," I said. Or maybe not. What if these people were building incredible things on their computers or gaming systems, much better things than I could make with my own two hands? I'd gotten much better at building since meeting Maison, though I still wasn't that good. However, I was even worse when it came to those annoying potions.

But that's when we heard Dad making his way to the tree house. He was holding his diamond sword and also had his tool pouch and a bag full of emeralds he'd mined.

"Stevie!" he called up to me when he got close. "I'm getting ready to go to the village and trade my emeralds with the blacksmith. I'll be back before it gets dark. Are you and Maison going to be okay?"

"We're fine," I called down. "We're just making stone swords."

"Are you memorizing your potions?" Dad wanted to know. Sometimes he really had a one-track mind.

"We will when we're done in the tree house!" I promised. I didn't tell him how long we would be in the tree house. I figured I could get a few minutes of studying in before Dad returned.

"See that you do!" Dad yelled. "Do you remember why we need to memorize potions?"

I stifled my sigh. Dad asked me that same question every single day. Even though I hadn't memorized all the potions, I'd memorized the answer to why-are-potions-so-important-Stevie?

"Because it sometimes takes more than a sword when danger arises," I rattled off. Dad's words. Exactly. "Even diamond swords have their pitfalls. If I or someone else is in danger, it is my duty as a citizen of the Overworld to help others. That includes the possibility of using potions."

"There you go," Dad said with a nod. Sometimes I think he just liked hearing himself quoted back. "And why must we always help others?"

"Because it's the right thing to do," I said.

"You're stealing that line from me," Maison whispered, since she'd said the same thing to the woman on the video.

"No, I'm not," I whispered back. "That's actually how he words it, too!"

I think Dad would have lectured me more on the importance of potions, but Maison being there threw him off. He was glad I had a friend, but he didn't know what to make of Maison. It wasn't that he didn't like her or anything. It was more that he still couldn't quite get his head wrapped around the fact that his son had found a portal to a world even he didn't know about. Dad liked to think he knew about everything there was to know in these parts.

Dad was also kind of uneasy about leaving us alone for a few hours, but he had nothing to worry about. It was a clear-skied day, and mobs were only dangerous after dark or if there was enough cloud cover to block out the sunlight.

"We'll be fine!" I called. "See you, Dad!"

"All right," Dad said gruffly. "You kids take care and I'll see you in a few hours." He hefted his diamond sword higher and began walking in the direction of the village.

"That's one thing that's nice about your world," I said to Maison with a sigh, leaning back. I'd finished my stone sword and Dad was way out of earshot now. I gave him extra, extra time to get out of earshot because I didn't want him overhearing this. "I wouldn't have to memorize all the ingredients in a potion because I could just look them up on the computer."

"That's not how it works, Stevie," Maison said, but that got a little smile from her. "It's good to know things on your own."

"I've seen you look up potions online while you're playing *Minecraft*," I said.

"Yeah, but that's for *playing*," she said. "*Minecraft* is real life for you."

I wanted to make a face, but I couldn't argue. "I know," I said. "It's just hard sometimes with my dad. He wants me to memorize all this stuff like I'm adult. Then he treats me as if I need to be constantly watched and lectured, like a kid who can't handle things."

"We're not being constantly watched," Maison pointed out. "He's going to the village."

"That's because he knows nothing bad is going to happen during the daylight," I said. "If it were dark, he'd send you home to your world and he'd make me study potions with him again."

Maison examined the stone sword she'd made, turning it over in the light. "Maybe we can both study your potions," she said. "I haven't memorized them all, either, and it'd be easier when I play *Minecraft* if I don't have to look them up every time."

"I don't know . . ." I said.

"And it'd be a good surprise for your dad if he found out we'd learned so much," she went on.

Memorizing potions sounded like a drag, though I realized it might be the distraction Maison needed. The Maison I knew was smart and fun, not scared and uneasy.

"All right," I said, sitting up. "Let's go."

And that's when everything went black.

CHAPTER 3

MAISON GASPED AND WE BOTH JUMPED UP, clutching our stone swords to our bodies. The whole Overworld had turned to night in an instant, no sunset or anything, and all of this was happening hours before it was supposed to. Overhead, a square moon shone down, giving us our only light except for the torches around the tree house.

"Has this ever happened before?" Maison asked in a worried voice.

"No," I said.

"Maybe it's a solar eclipse," she said. "Those happen in our world when the moon is between the earth and the sun and it covers up the sun for a little bit. Do you have eclipses in the Overworld?"

Quickly my brain rushed through years of knowledge Dad had given me. I unlocked information on mining, farming, reading, fighting mobs, all sorts of stuff. I couldn't think of anything about eclipses. I didn't even know the word.

"I don't think so," I said frailly. But I held on to the idea that maybe Maison was right, because I couldn't think of any other explanation. "How long do solar eclipses last?"

"Um, I don't know," Maison said. "I think it depends . . ."

I strained my ears, listening in on the darkness. If zombies were around, I'd hear them moaning in the distance. So far, nothing. But maybe a creeper was underneath, silently waiting for us, ready to blow up. I'd had some bad luck with creepers in the past, so I was especially nervous about them.

"What should we do?" I asked, my mouth dry.

"I was going to ask you that!" she said.

I weighed our options. The best bet was for Dad to come back and tell us what to do, but unless he showed up, that wasn't a choice. He'd probably reached the village by now. We could wait in the tree house until he came back or until it got light out. Most mobs couldn't bother us up this high . . . *most* mobs.

We could make a run for it and try to get back to the house. Dad had iron doors to protect us, and torches to keep mobs from spawning nearby. Plus, our cat, Ossie, wouldn't let any creepers close because creepers were scared of cats. The house would be safer than the tree house . . . if we could get there.

The house was just out of sight from the tree house, but right then it felt as if it couldn't be farther away.

"I think we should probably wait for my dad," I said. I pictured Dad reaching the village, seeing night come on, and hurrying back to get us. If he escorted us back to the house it'd still be intimidating, but I wouldn't be worried that we'd get hurt on our way. Dad was a master mob fighter.

Maison and I slowly sat down. Both of us were clutching our stone swords pretty tightly and listening to the night.

"There's a way you can turn *Minecraft* to night playing the game," Maison was musing to herself. "But I don't see how . . ."

We both heard a sound in the distance. And we both froze.

A person's voice. No, two! We weren't hearing zombie moans, so that was a relief. I didn't recognize the voices, but they didn't sound worried. They sounded like two people taking a stroll through the dark as if it were no big deal.

As they got closer, we could make out the voices a little better. Maison and I peered out over the balcony of the tree house, trying to get a good look. Two figures could just barely be seen in the distance, one taller than the other. They weren't shaped right—not blocky like people should be. But they weren't Endermen, even though that one figure was kind of tall. Definitely not creepers. Skeletons and other mobs could not talk, anyway.

One of the voices began to laugh. It was a boy's voice, but it didn't sound like a ha-ha-ha laugh, as if something were funny. The other voice, which I could now tell was a girl's, said something in response, and she definitely wasn't laughing.

"Are those villagers?" Maison asked.

"They can't be," I said. "They're not shaped right."

They were shaped more like . . . but no, that couldn't be.

I looked to Maison. In the moonlight, I could see her eyes widen, and she seemed to be having the same thoughts I was.

"They're people from your world," I said.

She covered her mouth with her hand. "That's not possible. They couldn't have found my portal."

"Maybe they opened another portal?" I suggested.

But as the people walked closer and the moonlight brought out their features, there could be no doubt that these were humans from Maison's world. The girl was toying uneasily with a necklace hanging from her neck, and the boy was taking bigger strides, smiling so that silver rays from the moon caught on his teeth like fangs. They were both dressed in dark clothing as if they wanted to blend in well with the night. The girl looked maybe a little older than Maison and me, but the tall boy looked more like he was a few years older, like seventeen or something.

They stopped by the tree house and looked up at us.

"Well, hullo there!" the boy said cheerfully. "Imagine seeing you this fine night!"

I was already surprised enough to see him, but his good mood surprised me more. Didn't he realize he was risking his life being out at night without a weapon to defend himself? I called, "Hello! Do you want to come up in the tree house with us? I can tell you're not from around here, but it gets dangerous at night."

The boy laughed as if I'd said something really cute. "Ha-ha, I don't think it's really night, now is it?" he teased. "You should come down here and we'll introduce ourselves. Don't worry, there are no creepers or anything around. I checked."

I looked to Maison, at a loss.

"They must not understand the danger," Maison said, squinting. "I don't know the guy, but the girl seems familiar somehow."

I looked back down at them. The girl didn't ring any bells to me.

"I think we better go down and explain to them why they should get up in the tree house with us," I said. "I don't want to scare them, but it's really not safe down there."

Slowly, cautiously, holding our stone swords at the ready, Maison and I climbed down to meet with the two people. When we had our feet on the ground, I turned to them and said, "Did you find a portal here?"

"We'll worry about details later, Stevie," the boy said with a wave of his hand.

"Well, for now, we really should get into the tree house for safety," I said. "I think my dad should be on his way right now, and he'll take us back to the house where we'll be safe." Then I stopped in my tracks. "Wait. How did you know my name? Did one of the village kids tell you?"

When he smiled this time, I really didn't like it. "I did just come from the village, but that's not how I know your name." He turned to the girl. "Would you like to tell them?" he asked her.

"No," she said in a tight voice.

"All right." He turned back to us and gave a sweeping bow. "You are Stevie and Maison, I presume?"

Maison clutched her sword tighter, her whole body tensing.

"Surprised?" the boy said. "You shouldn't be. And I think you'll find our names familiar as well." He gestured to the girl next to him. "This is DestinyIsChoice123." And he laid one hand on his chest, his hand pale as a skeleton's against the dark clothes and moonlight. "And I'm TheVampireDragon555."

CHAPTER 4

WAS SO SHOCKED ALL THAT CAME OUT OF MY MOUTH was a choking sound. "No," Maison was saying, shaking her head. "No, that can't be."

"Oh, but it is," TheVampireDragon555 said. His smile looked more like a sneer now. "I bet you'd like to know how this happened? Well, you can all thank Destiny here."

"No, please," the girl said in a low, pleading voice.

"Destiny!" Maison said. "That's how I know you! You're a seventh grader at my school!"

Destiny tried to back up into the shadows as if to hide herself. TheVampireDragon555 caught her by the arm and held her in place.

"Destiny is my cousin," he said. "And she had a very interesting story about zombies and spiders attacking her school. And of our little Ms. Maison, who supposedly saved the day."

I looked at Maison. Her expression had turned from fear to a growing anger, her eyes glaring at him. "That doesn't explain how you got here," she said.

"Oh, I'm getting to that," TheVampireDragon555 said. He appeared to be relishing every moment. "I knew your whole story about a cousin Stevie had to be made-up. And 'Cousin Stevie' and the mobs looked waaaay too much like *Minecraft* characters to be a co-incidence. I had Destiny do some searching. She snuck out paperwork about you from the school office after she faked a sore throat with the nurse. She got your home address."

Maison looked outraged. "You have no right to that!"

Not missing a beat, TheVampireDragon555 went on. "She learned when your baseball practice was. As soon as you were gone, she pretended to be a school friend working on a project with you. She told your mom that she'd left some homework in your bedroom, and could she please retrieve it?"

"Please, stop," Destiny said again, frailly.

"She got on your computer and got all the import-ant numbers, which she passed on to me," The Vampire-Dragon555 said. "First I thought I'd just have to hack your e-mail and see if you had any information in there. I couldn't find anything. But hacking e-mails is child's play. And come to find out, eleven-year-old 'heroes' aren't smart enough to know about having a firewall to pro-tect themselves. I broke into your computer's database, turned your *Minecraft* game into a multi-player game, and let myself in."

"No," Maison breathed, realizing.

"And I found a portal!" TheVampireDragon555 said dramatically, raising his hands toward the dark sky. "It was better than anything I could have dreamed! I found a portal to the Overworld, the real-live Overworld! I've been coming in and out of the Overworld for a week now, getting to know the landscape. I found the nearby village and I even tracked down where dear 'Cousin Stevie' lives."

"You—you—" I couldn't even get the words out. I didn't understand all this stuff about hacking or databases, but I understood enough to know that he'd gotten into Maison's private stuff. And that we were all in very real, immediate danger.

"What do you want?" Maison demanded.

"Well, I kind of feel like a kid in a candy store," TheVampireDragon555 said. "I've been griefing people on *Minecraft* games and trolling people online for years. But this! This is real!"

I found my voice. "My dad is going to be back any minute from the village," I said. "He has a diamond sword and he's not going to stand for any of this."

Come on, Dad! I was thinking. I figured he'd had enough time to get here from the village by now. What was taking him so long?

"Oh, you're talking about 'The Steve,'" TheVampireDragon555 said knowingly. "I heard people speaking about him when I was scouting out the village earlier. They say your dad's the most feared zombie slayer around. Well, I think he's going to be pretty busy for tonight. Wait, what am I saying, tonight? I mean for eternity!"

"This isn't right," Destiny said, tugging at his arm. "We have to stop this now."

"Oh, quit being such a party pooper," TheVampire-Dragon555 said, shaking her off his arm. Turning back to us, he explained, "You're probably wondering why it's dark out. It's really simple. I have control of Maison's *Minecraft* game now, and I used coding to turn it to night. And I plan to keep it this way. Forever."

"You can't!" I blurted out. "It's too dangerous!"

And then I stopped, realizing how stupid I sounded. He wasn't afraid because he *wanted* eternal night with mobs constantly on the prowl.

"I don't mean to toot my own horn, but I know a lot about codes," TheVampireDragon555 said. "If you don't believe me, look behind you."

But he didn't need to say it. I could already hear the moaning of zombies as they approached.

CHAPTER 5

MAISON AND I WHIRLED AROUND, OUR SWORDS at the ready. At first there was only the terrible moaning, the sign that zombies were on their way. And then, out of the darkness, ten zombies appeared, arms outstretched, their blank, black eyes fixed on us.

I charged the closest one, slamming through it with my stone sword, putting all my strength into it. The zombie stumbled back, shook, and moved toward me again, moaning. I flung my sword and hit it against the zombie. Beside me, Maison thrust her stone sword into a zombie, momentarily stalling it. As soon as it shook itself off, it was moving toward her again.

"With proper coding, it's really easy to create zombies wherever I want!" TheVampireDragon555 called to us over the sounds of moaning zombies and swinging swords. He was watching us with his arms crossed and a smile on his face. "But you guys really shouldn't have too much to worry about here. You took on a lot more zombies at the middle school."

We *had* taken on a lot more mobs at Maison's school, but we'd also had a lot more help from teachers and students. Maison and I stepped close together, swords out, tensing as more mobs approached.

"Now!" I said. Both Maison and I burst out, hitting the zombies.

Destiny turned toward TheVampireDragon555. "You have to call off the zombies!" she shouted at him. "I didn't agree to this!"

"Oh, they're fine," TheVampireDragon555 said, as if Maison and I were in the middle of a really simple job. "Besides, there are only two zombies left now."

"This is wrong!" Destiny said loudly. "I don't care what you say. I'm going back and I'm—"

"Do you know what I think, Destiny?" TheVampireDragon555 cut her off. "I think now that we're in the Overworld, you're no longer of any use to me."

And he shoved her into the arms of a zombie.

CHAPTER 6

I RAN TO TRY TO STOP THE ZOMBIE FROM GETTING HER, but it was already too late. I heard a zombie's moan, a girl's scream, and then Destiny fell to her knees on the ground, trembling and choking, her head thrown forward so her long hair covered her face.

Bellowing in shock, I leapt up and stabbed the zombie that had gotten her, then stabbed it again. It vanished into the eternal night at the same time Maison took out the other remaining zombie.

TheVampireDragon555 chuckled lightly. "Being a zombie is a perfect career for you, Destiny," he mocked her shaking form. "You never could do things on your own. You always had to follow someone else's lead. Well, you know what? Your choice in following me around wasn't exactly your smartest decision, huh?"

"How . . . how could you . . ." her voice croaked.

"What did you say?" TheVampireDragon555's smile had disappeared.

"How . . . could . . ." The croak in her voice was slightly louder now.

Destiny slowly, shakingly rose to her now-grotesque feet. Her hair fell back in place, but her skin had turned a rotten green. Her eyes were a deep, dark red, and they showed how stunned and shocked she was. Then her chapped lips cracked open and she gurgled in that strange, otherworldly voice, "You pushed me right into that zombie."

TheVampireDragon555 bent in front of her. "You can talk!" he said, spellbound. He seemed to be really thinking through what all of this might mean.

This impossible night was becoming even more impossible: zombies could never talk! Every now and then a zombie attack on a village would go bad, and we'd end up with zombie villagers. They'd still look like themselves, only with green skin and red eyes, but here's the thing: even they couldn't talk. It didn't matter that they'd been human before. Once they'd been bitten and turned, they could only moan and wander mindlessly.

"Say something," TheVampireDragon555 coaxed. "What is the square root of eighty-one? What is the closest planet to earth? How many fingers am I holding up?"

Destiny looked at him with uncertainty. Her cracked lips parted again. "Nine," she rasped. "Mars. Four fingers."

TheVampireDragon555 took a step back as if he were scared Destiny might burn him. At the same time, he was fascinated by what she had turned into.

Three more zombies appeared out of the darkness then and Maison and I readied our swords, but TheVampireDragon555 and Destiny were too distracted to pay much attention.

"Did I code something wrong?" I heard TheVampireDragon555 murmur to himself. Maison and I rushed to take care of the new zombies while he continued to talk to himself. "No, no code. Couldn't be. It must be . . . it must be because we're not from this world. Our bodies respond differently. We keep our minds. We . . ."

He stopped talking, deep in thought. As I battled one of the zombies, I got a glimpse of TheVampireDragon555 over the zombie's shoulder. A dark cloud had gone over his eyes as he took on the real meaning of this. I realized what he was going to do, but by the time I did, it was too late to reach him.

He threw himself into the arms of one of the zombies.

"Stop him!" Maison screamed.

Maison and I each destroyed the zombie in front of us, but neither of us had time to get to the third zombie, the one TheVampireDragon555 went to. TheVampireDragon555 fell against the zombie, and this time, instead of a scream we heard laughter, a shrieking laughter that echoed over the vast landscape.

CHAPTER 7

MAISON AND I JUMPED FORWARD AND STABBED the last zombie. It disappeared, but the damage was done. TheVampireDragon555 dropped to his feet, trembling, overpowered by the change coming over him. He had his hands clutched in his hair as he was bent there, the long fingers changing from skeleton pale to zombie green under the moonlight.

Then slowly, with legs that were gradually growing more steady, he stood up to his full height, towering above us. He still wasn't a vampire or a dragon, but he was most definitely a zombie now. He opened his mouth and said, "Perfect. It worked just the way I wanted it to."

Destiny gaped at him. "What have you done?"

"The only thing that makes sense," he replied, flexing his hands and finding they still worked just fine. "I was going to keep myself clear of zombies and just let them attack the people here. But look at this! I still have my human mind, plus all the powers of a zombie."

He turned and grinned hungrily at Maison and me.

Maison poised her sword out at him. "You're still just a zombie," she said fiercely. "Stevie and I know how to handle zombies. Don't we, Stevie?"

It probably would have been helpful if I'd given a brave, "We sure do!" answer right then. But I was struck speechless. I didn't know how to handle this. I didn't know how to handle *any* of this.

"You can put that sword away," TheVampireDragon555 told Maison coolly. He was eyeing her stone sword as if it was some silly little toy that couldn't do anything. "I'm not going to attack you. At least not yet, anyway."

"What do you want, VampireDragon?" Maison demanded. "You found me. Aren't I the one you want?"

"Of course I don't want you," TheVampireDragon555 said. He sounded offended that Maison had thought that. "Destiny's the one who has a grudge against you. Me, I just wanted to figure out where all those zombies came from."

"What do you mean?" I gasped.

"Trolling people online gets boring after so many years," TheVampireDragon555 said. "I hurt their feelings, I probably make them cry, yeah, yeah, yeah. They could just ignore it if they weren't so sensitive. But here . . . here I can really troll and grief. Here, you can't just turn off your computer to get away from me." A dark expression came over his face. "Tonight is where the fun begins."

"We have to get to the village!" I whispered in Maison's ear. "We have to warn them and get my dad!"

She nodded, her eyes not leaving TheVampire-Dragon555.

"I know what you're thinking," TheVampireDragon555 said. "It won't do any good for you to warn the villagers, I can promise you that. But I'm not going to stop you. Go, go."

Maison and I only looked at each other for an instant. And then we were running, running as fast as we could toward the village.

CHAPTER 8

IT WAS A TERRIBLE SIGHT THAT AWAITED US.

"No!" I exclaimed. "Where are the iron golems?"

Iron golems are meant to protect the village, but they were nowhere in sight. Had TheVampireDragon555 removed them somehow with his computer codes? He'd definitely put something else in their place: the village was overrun with zombies, their moans and hisses filling the air. On top of that, some of the buildings were on fire. Yellow and jack-o-lantern-tinted flames roared out of broken windows and colored the sky.

Maison was beside me, gasping for breath. "Where are the villagers? Are they hiding in their houses?"

My eyes scanned the buildings. There was a villager— with green skin! There was another one, and another, and another— and they all had green skin!

"It's too late," I said. "The villagers have already turned. They weren't prepared, with the iron golems gone and the sudden night."

Now I knew Dad really was our only hope left. He was probably here somewhere in the maze of buildings, fighting off zombies and rescuing people. That would explain why he hadn't made it back to the tree house yet. If zombies had been unleashed on the village, he'd save the village first, figuring Maison and I were much safer up in our tree house and far away from all this madness.

But how would we find him without being attacked by zombies? What if we went into one section of the village and he was in another? What if we went in just as he was going out? In Maison's world, they had cell phones where people could talk to one another in an instant, no matter where they were. In our world, we didn't have anything that useful for situations like this.

"Dad!" I shouted at the top of my lungs, hoping he was close enough to hear me. Sometimes Dad almost seemed superhuman because he was so good at solving problems. For all I knew, he had super-hearing, or some sort of magical device in his brain that would tell him when his son was in trouble. "Dad!"

"I think we might have to go in there," Maison said. "But I don't know how we can get in and come back out without . . . without . . ."

Without turning into zombies, I said in my head for her.

"Maybe we can run around the edges of the village," I said. "And keep calling him that way?" Then I saw a familiar shape in the crowd in the village. It was the blacksmith! But when he turned his head, I saw the greenness of his face and my stomach dropped. I knew that Dad was supposed to be with the blacksmith today.

Maybe the zombies got here before Dad reached the blacksmith, I thought desperately. *There's no way Dad would let the blacksmith get hurt if he was there.*

Maison and I began to rush along the edges of the village, with me shouting, "Dad!" while she shouted, "Steve!" The more we had to shout, the more our voices hurt from the screaming and the smoke. And the more desperate we sounded.

"Stevie! Maison!" a boy's voice called from behind us.

We turned, but it was only TheVampireDragon555, calmly making his way up toward the village. Destiny was nowhere to be seen.

"I forgot to mention one teensy weensy detail," TheVampireDragon555 said. "You can't warn the villagers because I already used codes to unleash a bunch of zombies on them. Oops, that was probably an important detail to tell you. Oh, and I took care of the iron golems, too. They were in my way."

And that's when I just snapped.

"You did this!" I yelled, coming at him.

He held up one green hand, palm out, signaling me to stop. "I wouldn't come closer if I were you," he said.

"Why?" I said. This bully wasn't going to harass Maison online, break into our world, turn it into night, and set zombies loose on the villagers. And somehow, what made it worst of all was how pleased he seemed during it. At least zombies attacked mindlessly because it was their nature. TheVampireDragon555 was in full control of what he was doing.

"Are you going to bite me?" I demanded. "You don't have a sword. Maison and I will stop you with our swords before you even get close to us."

"Ooh, you sound violent," he said, enjoying this.

"No, you're violent!" I said. "We're just trying to protect ourselves. I only fight when there's no other choice for our safety."

"How noble," TheVampireDragon555 said, making it sound like a bad thing. "But you never let me finish what I was saying. It turns out keeping my brain isn't the only amazing thing that happens to people like Destiny and me when we get bitten by zombies in the Overworld." He paused for dramatic effect. "I've been doing some experimenting with my powers, and it seems we also have powers over zombies."

"Powers over zombies?" Maison repeated, a hitch of fear in her voice.

"Yes, watch," said TheVampireDragon555. He turned to a group of zombie villagers in earshot of us. "You seven!"

The seven zombie villagers turned their dark red eyes on him.

"Get them!" TheVampireDragon ordered, pointing toward Maison and me. "Get them by any means necessary! Don't let them escape!"

At once, the zombies obeyed, lurching toward us.

CHAPTER 9

"**R**UN!" MAISON SAID.

"Zombies!" TheVampireDragon555 hollered, catching the attention of zombies farther down. They all looked toward him. "Get those two!"

Zombies were coming at us from all directions but one. Seeing we had no other choice, Maison and I took off down a street into the village, the zombies at our heels. But as we turned down that street, more zombies popped out of the buildings in front of us.

We skidded to a stop, panicked, and dove into one of the buildings. Maison slammed the door shut. However, it wasn't an iron door, just a wooden one, and the zombies began to pound on it. I knew it wouldn't take long for them to break through.

"Quickly!" I said. We ran across the building to the other side of it. There was an open window we could squeeze through. I put my head out the window, looked in both directions, and said, "It's safe." For the moment, anyway.

Just then the front door gave way and the zombies broke in, moaning. I jumped on the windowsill and pulled myself out, Maison a second behind me. Our feet hit the ground outside.

"Which way?" Maison gasped.

"I think we need to get out of the village," I said.

"What about your dad?"

Wildly, I shook my head. I didn't even know where to begin looking for him. Our only hope was to flee from here. It's not as if we could save the village, anyway. Not two people against all these zombies, not two kids with stone swords.

"He's probably headed back home," I said. At this rate, he would also see that the village was a lost cause and he had to get reinforcements elsewhere. The tree house was on the way home. He'd see we weren't there and continue on to the house to make sure we were safe and then find people from other villages to help.

Hissing, a zombie reached its arm out of the window and swung for us, barely missing. That was all the motivation we needed. Maison and I turned down the street, racing to get out of the village.

But we should have known it wouldn't be that easy. When we were just about to reach the end of the street, several zombies came out from hiding in the buildings. They had the exit blocked off.

"This way!" I said. We veered around, but zombies were behind us there, too. And none of the other buildings around us looked safe, either. Zombies were reaching out of windows toward us, clawing to open doors from the inside out.

"We're trapped!" Maison yelled. "We're going to have to fight our way out!"

I looked around, trying to figure out which batch of zombies would be the easiest to take out. More zombies were by the exit of the village, so we couldn't go that way. Only three zombies were on the street if we went deeper into the village. It wouldn't help us in our mission to get out of the village, but going deeper in was our only option right then. We'd have to find another way out.

"Let's get them," I said.

Maison didn't need any more directions. We charged the zombies, hitting them square on, knocking them to the side. We didn't try to finish them off and make them disappear; we just needed to get past them. If we took the time to finish them off, that only gave the other zombies more time to surround us.

Once we knocked those zombies back, we skidded into an alleyway that was darker than the rest of the village.

"We'll loop around," I said, "if there aren't more on the other side!"

But I knew the odds of that. Turning out of the alleyway, we looked left and we looked right. Zombies on the left. Zombies on the right. Advancing on us. Moaning.

"The house!" I said. The house directly in front of us had no zombies in the windows. There still might be some inside, but it was our only hope.

Maison and I burst into the house, throwing the door shut behind us. She dragged some furniture against the door to create a swift, makeshift barricade. It would keep the zombies out longer, though not by much.

Again we reached for the window. And we couldn't believe what we saw outside.

No zombies! The street was dark and terrible, but there wasn't a mob in sight.

"I think we're going to make it," I said to Maison, panting. "We'll turn left, run a few streets, and we'll be out of the village."

I pulled myself out the window, balancing the sword. Maison followed a moment later. While trying to be as silent and quick as possible, we rushed down the inky black street, aware of the zombies a street away crying out for us.

I could see the plain green grass ahead, the grass that meant the end of the village. With each leaping bound of our feet, we were getting closer to the grass. A few more houses and we'd be there. A few more houses and we had a chance.

That's when the door in the house next to us exploded with a thunderous splintering. Shards of wood flew everywhere. I saw the swarm of zombies break through, so many of them that they were almost tripping over one another. The zombie in the front was the tallest and strongest looking of all, a diamond sword clutched in its hand. The sword swung out at me, straight at my head, and the only way for me to dodge it was to throw myself forward. I hit the ground with a thud, my stone sword flying from my hand and landing uselessly out of my reach.

I struggled to get on my feet, but it was too late. The big zombie stood over me, lifting its diamond sword high above its head. All I could do was flip over. I looked up into the big zombie's face, and even though the face was green, and even though it was transformed into a zombie's blank hunger, I would recognize him anywhere.

"Dad!" I cried, holding out my arm. "No!"

CHAPTER 10

EVERYTHING WAS GOING IN SLOW MOTION, AS IF I was outside of my body, watching the horror of the scene. Dad continued to raise his diamond sword, my words lost on him. Vaguely, I could see zombie villagers bursting out of the door of the house on the other side. They surrounded Maison, her sword slashing at them, but there were too many of them for a single person. It was over for her. It was over for me. TheVampire-Dragon555 had won. He had taken over the Overworld.

Then I heard a girl's voice from far in the distance. "STOP IT!" the voice yelled.

Dad froze over me, like he was trapped in a photograph. Maison had shown me photographs, how they capture an instant. All the zombies stopped moving, photograph-still.

For a moment I was still as they were. But it was only from shock, because then I realized I was blinking, so I could move. My heart was pounding. Maison pushed out of the zombie swarm that had surrounded her, and the swarm stayed as frozen as ever. She grabbed my stone sword where it had fallen on the ground.

"Stevie!" she said. "Are you okay?"

She was next to me, grabbing me under my arms, pulling me up to my feet. I couldn't stop looking at Dad, at his diamond sword in his hand. The moans of zombies could be heard in the distance, but not anywhere close to us. The streets around us had grown eerily silent.

"Stevie, let's go!" Maison said.

I was looking at Dad, at his green skin and blank stare. Then my eyes wandered to the diamond sword.

I couldn't just leave it here. He might be able to hurt other people with it. And in the mind-set he was in now, he might even accidentally nick himself. That sword was sharp.

And if I had that diamond sword, maybe I could . . .

My hand inched toward it. Dad didn't respond. My hand got closer. Was he going to unfreeze the second I touched the sword handle? What if getting this close made him snap back to reality and he attacked me again?

Maison didn't want to take any chances. "Stevie, run!" she shrilled, blaring in my ears.

I snatched the diamond sword out of Dad's hand. He didn't react and the sword moved easily into my grasp, letting me feel the weight of it. The responsibility of it.

I turned to Maison and the two of us bolted from the village. Behind us, we could hear the zombies, and before us, we could see only darkness.

CHAPTER 11

EVEN THOUGH WE RAN AS FAST AS WE COULD, IT was the longest trip back from the village ever. Dad's diamond sword was glinting blue in my hand, and I kept thinking, *We're doomed, we're trapped, it's all over for us now.* My ears were straining, trying to pick up the sound of any mobs that might be nearby. But as we got farther from the village, all I could hear was the sound of our pounding feet and the gasping of our breaths.

Then the tree house came into view, standing guard over the landscape like a fort. That meant the house wasn't much farther. And what was I going to do there? Grab my cat Ossie and move out into Maison's world, because that was the only option I had left? Because the Overworld was destroyed and no one could save it?

Now I got why Maison had been so scared. I thought those cyberbullies were just people typing mean things from anywhere. I didn't realize they could actually affect anyone's personal life.

Finally I could see the house ahead! The torches were lit out front to protect us from mobs spawning, and Maison and I basically collapsed on the floor once we got inside the house, totally out of breath. Ossie, who was unaware of the world falling apart, came over to us, purring.

I dropped Dad's sword to the floor and covered my face with my hands, shaking and rocking to myself.

Meanwhile, Maison seized one of Dad's thick books from off the wall and threw it down on the crafting table, turning pages as fast as she could. "Stevie!" she said. "We have to turn the zombie villagers back into humans!"

"There's no point," I heard myself mumble.

She looked up sharply. "What do you mean?"

"I mean you were right," I said. "I should have listened to you from the beginning. I thought mean words on the computer weren't anything compared to mobs, but look . . ."

"Neither one of us ever could have expected this," she said. "But now we're the Overworld's only hope."

"No, the Overworld has no hope!" I snapped. "Don't you get it? So what if we turn the villagers back? The-VampireDragon555 will keep it night and keep making zombies. How do we fight against *that*?"

"There's got to be a way," Maison said earnestly. "What if we make enough potions to turn your dad and a few other people back? Then they can help us fight."

I shook my head. "My dad just tried to attack me with a sword," I said. "He's one of them now. He's not like people from your world who can keep their mind."

"And that's why we need a potion to change them back!" she insisted. "What's it called? The Potion of . . ."

There were a lot of potions Dad had been trying to drill into my head. The Potion of Night Vision. The Potion of Slowness. The Potion of Swiftness. "The Potion of Weakness," I said.

"The Potion of Weakness." She flipped harder through the pages. "What goes into it?"

"Oh . . . uh . . . uh . . ." I racked my brain. "Well, first you need to . . . uh . . ." *Jeez, Stevie, you should know this!* "You need to make three glass bottles on the crafting table and put water in them."

"Okay, that sounds easy."

"Next you create a brewing stand. So you get a blaze rod and some cobblestones for that. Then you have to ferment a spider eye. You ferment a spider eye with a mushroom and . . . and . . . Oh, I don't remember!"

Maison flipped through and found the right page. As she ran her finger under the words, she said, "You ferment the spider eye with a mushroom and sugar and then you brew it. For the last piece, you need some gunpowder. Do you have supplies like that here?"

One good thing about Dad: he kept tons of things in storage.

"We'll have at least some of all those things," I said. "But I don't know if we have enough to change the whole village back."

Maison kept reading. "It says here that the Potion of Weakness by itself isn't enough to change a zombie villager back into a villager. You also have to give them each a golden apple. For each golden apple, you need one apple and nine golden nuggets."

I hit my hand hard against the floor. We definitely didn't have enough gold or enough apples to make this work. We'd only be able to save a few people. And despite what Maison thought, I was convinced that even this wouldn't do much good. As soon as we saved someone, TheVampireDragon555 would probably pop up out of nowhere and order more zombies to sic us.

"Then we'll just need to get more gold and apples," Maison said. "Where are the closest apple trees around here?"

"Apples don't grow on apple trees," I said.

"Of course they do," she said. "That's why they're apple trees."

"No," I said. "Apples come from oak trees in the Overworld, remember?" We'd been over this before when Maison showed me the apple tree in her yard and I told her it was weird that apples grew on apple trees. She'd told me it was weird that in my world apples didn't grow on apple trees.

"There's one oak tree that I used to get wood for the tree house, but my dad and I already picked most of the apples from it," I said. "And my dad has some gold, but if we want more, we'd have to go mining, and then who knows if we'd find any? Plus, if each zombie villager needs eight golden nuggets just so we can make a golden apple, then . . ."

I tried doing some math in my head. I didn't like the big numbers I was coming up with.

"I think we need to go to the portal and get out of here," I said.

"No!" Maison said. "We've done this before. We can do it again."

"That was different!" I said. "We were fighting zombies in the school. Just regular zombies! Not zombies that obey orders, not human zombies that give orders! We weren't in eternal night, and we weren't in a world where you can make more zombies appear by coding!"

Maison watched my outburst, stunned. "You're just going to give up?" she said in shock.

I looked at the floor because it was better than looking at the hurt in her eyes. "I don't want to give up," I said. "But I don't know what choice we have."

Right then, there was a heavy knocking on the door.

CHAPTER 12

MY HEAD JERKED UP. BOTH MAISON AND I stared at the door, frozen. Had TheVampire-Dragon555 found us?

"Please, open up!" called a weak, cracking voice. "Please!"

Maison and I looked at each other in disbelief. I picked up the diamond sword. Grabbing her stone sword, Maison inched closer to the door, her weapon poised in case she needed it. The person was still pounding at the door. Hesitantly, Maison pressed the button for the door to open, and there stood Destiny.

"You!" Maison said, eyes flashing.

"Please, I want to help you," Destiny said. Her voice still croaked a little, like a zombie's hiss was trying to take over her normal voice.

"Likely story," Maison said, and began to close the door.

"Wait!" Destiny put her hand in the doorway to stop it. "Give me a chance. I can explain everything."

Destiny looked at me as if I would defend her from Maison. But I wasn't buying it, either. I thought Destiny had a lot of nerve showing up here after everything.

"You're the one who helped TheVampireDragon555 break into the Overworld!" I said.

She put her head down. "Yes," she said softly. "I did. But I didn't know that it would go this far."

"How far did you expect it to go?" Maison demanded. "I saw the nasty things you wrote about me online. All the threats. Saying you were going to come and get me? You can't just show up and play innocent!"

Destiny bit at the edges of her fingers. No, actually, she was biting the nails on them, as if they were some kind of food. Did zombies from Maison's world eat their own fingers? There were blotches of black on her nails, which must have been some other weird thing that happened to zombies from Maison's world.

"I'm sorry," Destiny said. "If you can just let me in . . ."

"Why?" Maison said. "So you can bite us and turn us into zombies?"

The room was so tense you could have cut the air with a knife. That's when Ossie, who Dad always said was an excellent judge of character, strolled over to Destiny and began to rub against her legs, purring. I couldn't believe it. Maison couldn't believe it, either.

"Ossie, no!" I said, wanting the silly cat to back away. I'd already lost my world and my dad; I didn't need Destiny hurting my cat, too. I winced when Destiny reached down, but all she did was pick Ossie up and cradle her, rubbing the cat under the chin so that she purred extra, extra hard.

"I want to help you turn the villagers back and stop TheVampireDragon555," Destiny said. "He's not the only one who can order the zombies around. I was the one who ordered them off you so you could escape from the village."

CHAPTER 13

THE ONLY SOUND IN THE ROOM WAS OSSIE'S LOUD purring. Maison and I were gaping.

Of course! I thought. *The girl's voice in the distance. The way the zombies all froze.* Dad had had his sword mid-air, ready to use it, so there had to have been a logical reason for why he had stopped. It wasn't because he'd recognized me—he was too far gone to recognize me.

However, Maison wasn't won over so quickly.

"How do we know you're telling the truth?" she wanted to know.

"I did hear a voice," I told Maison.

"Do you know for sure it was her voice?" Maison asked.

I shook my head. It had been too far away for me to tell if it had that distinctive crack to it. But who else would have been able to order zombies around? What Destiny said made sense.

"Look, I'll come clean, I'll tell you everything," Destiny said.

"All right," Maison said, testy. "For starters, why do you hate me?"

Destiny sucked in air as if those words had knocked the wind out of her. I could tell she wasn't ready for that question, though I thought it was a pretty reasonable question for Maison to ask.

"I don't . . . I don't hate you," Destiny said, looking at Ossie instead of Maison.

Maison snorted.

"I wanted to *be* you," Destiny said. "I saw how much the other kids picked on you at the beginning of the school year. They picked on me, too. I always eat alone at lunch. No one wants to pick me to be their partner for class projects. Someone wrote nasty things about me on the walls in the girls' bathroom and the school didn't care. They just told me it could have been about the word 'destiny' and I shouldn't point fingers at people."

Destiny sighed. "It probably sounds dumb, but I almost felt like we had an invisible friendship because we were both alone. I saw the boys bugging you, and it was a relief because it got them off my back. I'd look at you alone in the cafeteria and you'd always be working on something, like a little house or a science project. I knew you must have felt lonely, but you were doing the best you could in a bad situation. I kept promising myself one day I would talk to you, though I was too scared and it never happened. I even wrote some notes to pass over to you, but I couldn't even get up the courage to pass them."

I looked over at Maison. Her dark eyes were unreadable, yet she wasn't clutching her sword as hard.

"I noticed you were into *Minecraft*," Destiny went on. "I am, too. Then one day I was in the auditorium for an assembly on safety, and all these zombies and large spiders showed up. They looked just like the mobs in *Minecraft*! You were there, too, Stevie. Then you two led the school in a fight against the mobs, and the next thing I knew, Maison was a hero. She was all over the news. People wanted to interview her. She won awards from the city. Bullies stopped teasing her. She was the hero of the school, and I was still . . . forgotten."

"I don't see what this—" Maison began.

"No, you wouldn't," Destiny interrupted. "I was thinking that you must have noticed that I was alone, too, so now that you were popular, you'd let me hang out and I wouldn't have to be a loner anymore. Because you know what it feels like to be pushed around and ignored. But you never even glanced at me. Ever.

"I went home one night and cried," she continued. "My cousin was over visiting and when I told him what happened, he wanted to know more. He was already obsessed with you, Maison. He knew about you from the news and he was excited to learn my connection to you. He's been trolling people for years, and he got stuck on you because he thought you were the key to finding out where all the zombies had come from—"

"Wait," I interrupted her. "What's trolling?" That was a word I kept hearing and I didn't know what it meant.

"It's when you say and do things on purpose to hurt people's feelings online," Destiny said. "My cousin has made a real, uh, hobby out of it. He started showing me how to do it. You just make up an online name and you can say or do whatever you want. At first I really enjoyed it! I shouldn't have said those things about you, Maison, but they felt good to say at the time. They made me feel powerful, like no one could stop me. And no one knew what I was doing online, so no one could stop me!"

She licked her green, chapped lips. "But my cousin wanted more. He told me it would be really funny if he could hack into your e-mail. He thought he might find some embarrassing stuff on you there. I found your home address at the school and talked your mom into letting me in your room. I was in and out in a few minutes. I gave your information to my cousin, and the next time I saw him, he was super excited. He said, 'In your wildest dreams, you wouldn't believe what I found.'"

"The portal," I said.

"Exactly," she said. "I didn't believe it, but then he brought me here with him. He showed me around. At first, he was just planning to do some griefing. He loves griefing people when they play *Minecraft*."

"Griefing?" I asked.

"Messing up their games," Destiny explained. "Then he started playing around with codes and realized he could make things happen in the Overworld. Like spawning his own zombies. Or changing the world to night. He told me we were going to come in and mess around with you guys. But then he turned it night and released zombies on the village. I kept telling him this was wrong, but he said we were just getting started."

"I don't know," Maison said. "How do we know you're not a double agent?"

"Double agent?" I repeated. They were using a lot of terms I didn't know.

"That means she's really helping out TheVampire-Dragon555, and she's only pretending to be our friend," Maison said. "She's going to tell sad stories for us to feel sorry for her, then she's going to get information out of us and take it back to TheVampireDragon555."

I hadn't thought of that, but I realized Maison made a good point. Now I didn't know what to believe.

"You said that TheVampireDragon555 is your cousin, right?" Maison said. "So you'd support him over us."

Destiny shook her head. "He's my cousin, but we've never been friends. He's always been mean. He thinks it's funny to upset other people. When I was saying those mean things online, it made me feel powerful and safe, but I never thought it was funny. He writes mean things and laughs."

I thought about TheVampireDragon555's cruel laughter. Even though Destiny and TheVampireDragon555 had both started out harassing Maison online the same way, I could see they were both very different people.

But I didn't have long to think. Because then we all heard the sound of zombies moaning.

CHAPTER 14

OUTSIDE, ZOMBIES WERE LURCHING TOWARD US! WE were being so foolish, leaving the door open like that while we talked. Maison was right, Destiny was a double agent who'd led a whole village of zombies after us! Destiny turned and yelled at them, "Go away!"

Then I saw there were only three zombies, and they were regular zombies, not zombie villagers.

The zombies stopped. Then they turned and shuffled away, back into the night.

"Oh . . . my . . . gosh," Maison said.

So she wasn't a double agent? "Wait," I said. "Does this mean that we can just take you back to the village and you can order all the zombies to stop attacking us?"

Destiny gently set Ossie on the floor. "It's not that easy. TheVampireDragon555 showed up right after you got away, and he was furious. I told the zombies to stay put and he told them to move, and then they started moving. I don't get it. It's like they only listen to me when he's not around."

"I wonder why that could be," I mused, thinking hard.

"I don't know," she said. "For all I know, he's coded something weird. I think our best bet to turn the zombie villagers back is to make the Potion of Weakness and get golden apples."

Maison's eyebrows went up. "We were thinking the same thing."

"She was," I corrected, motioning toward Maison. "But I don't see what good it will do. Won't TheVampire-Dragon555 just turn them all back into zombies? And what about the eternal night thing?"

"The 'eternal' night isn't really eternal night," Destiny said. "He keeps setting the Overworld to night on his computer. It only lasts so long, and then he goes back through the portal to set it back again."

"So if we can keep him away from the computer . . ." Maison began.

"And that's not all," Destiny said. "I know what his plans are."

This time Maison made the gesture that Destiny could fully come into the house. Maison closed the door behind her.

"So his main thing is trolling," Destiny said. "That's why he let you get away the first time. He wanted you to see the village and be upset. Once you'd seen village, he didn't really care exactly what happened to you, as long as it was bad. That's why he told the zombies to go after you."

"What is he trying to accomplish?" Maison asked. "Like, what's the big picture for him?"

"That's the thing," Destiny said. "He likes wreaking havoc online. This is like a playground for him. He gets to use his computer to make real zombies and real night. At least real in this world. His only 'big picture' is attacking the Overworld. When I left the village, he was telling the zombies there that he was going to turn them into an army . . ."

My heart thumped so hard I thought everyone in the room must have heard it.

". . . and take them to every part of the Overworld," she said. "He was starting to assemble them. It's going to take him some time. So he's trying to get all the zombie villagers in order, and he's jumping back and forth between the portals."

"He can't keep that up for long," Maison said.

"No," Destiny agreed. "Once he gets the zombie villagers in order, he's going to come here after you, I guarantee it."

"So we don't have much time," I said.

"This is what I'm thinking," Destiny said. "We need to get someplace high, like the roof of this house, and we'll make Potions of Weakness. When he leads the zombie villagers here, we'll start splashing them with the potions and turn them back. If we can keep them all here long enough, he won't get a chance to run back to the portal. The sun will come back up and we can trap him."

"The tree house!" Maison said, and I remembered earlier how it had looked like a fort to me. "We'll go in the tree house with the potions!"

"There's just one problem," I said. "We don't have enough supplies to make all the potions and golden apples we'll need to save the villagers."

For the first time, Destiny smiled. "Oh, that's not a problem at all," she said. "Because, you see, I know computer codes, too."

CHAPTER 15

"THEVAMPIREDRAGON555 IS BETTER AT CODES THAN I am," Destiny said. "He's got it blocked so I can't undo what he's done, like the night thing. But I can go through the portal and make it rain apples. All the apples you need. I can get you gold, too. I know the right codes for whatever ingredients you want."

Maison and I looked wildly at each other.

"Is that true?" I asked.

"There are codes that can do stuff like that," Maison acknowledged. "I just don't know how they work."

"Tell me what you need," Destiny said, holding out her green hands.

I took her to the supply shed and showed her what we had. Destiny quickly began doing math in her head of how much we would need. "I'll make sure we get extra, just in case," she said.

"How are you going to do the codes?" I wanted to know.

"I'm going to have to go back out through the portal and get on TheVampireDragon555's computer," Destiny said.

"Is it safe?" I asked. Who knows how many mobs were out there between the house and the portal?

Maison had a totally different question. "Do we trust her?" she asked.

Destiny looked hurt. "If I'm risking my safety to get to the portal for you, doesn't that show you can trust me?" she asked.

That was a good point. I looked to Maison.

"Maybe," Maison said. "Or maybe you're going to run back to TheVampireDragon555 and tell him we don't have enough supplies so he might as well come get us now?"

My stomach soured that Maison might be right and I looked back to Destiny.

"I told you what I did was wrong!" Destiny pleaded, her dark red eyes earnest. "I told you why I did it, and I told you I changed."

"Here's something else I don't get," Maison said. "So TheVampireDragon555 got it so you can't undo the night thing, but he left it so you're able to make supplies? Wouldn't he think through that and block you from doing anything?"

Maison was really thinking through everything.

"He started to block different things, including the night part," Destiny said. "But then he got anxious and wanted to get going, because he could see from his computer that Stevie's dad had gone to the village and you and Stevie were alone in the tree house. He thought it was the perfect time to attack."

Well, that might explain it. But Maison still wasn't impressed.

"You almost sound too brave, offering to run out like that," Maison said. "Even if you're a zombie, you might still get attacked. You don't even have a weapon. And how come earlier you were so mad at TheVampireDragon555, then as soon as you turned into a zombie, you stopped being angry and just answered his questions?"

Destiny appeared stunned to be asked this. "I was in *shock*," she said. "How do you think you'd feel if you suddenly turned into a zombie?"

Destiny looked at Maison for a long moment, and then slowly reached into the pocket of her pants. Maison and I both cringed, expecting her to pull out some kind of weapon. But when her hand came back into view, she was holding a few ratty-looking papers.

"Here are the notes I couldn't pass to you," Destiny said softly. I was so used to zombies looking big and scary, but even with her green skin and red eyes, she just looked so lost and sad.

The papers were all wadded and folded and Maison slowly began un-wadding and unfolding them. "'Dear Maison,'" she read out loud. "'I'm writing this because I'm too scared to talk to you. I think we should be friends. I don't think we'd be so lonely anymore.'"

She unfolded another paper and started to read. "'Dear Maison, how are you today? I noticed some kids pushed you around again. They've done the same to me.

Maybe we can hang out at lunch and they'll leave us alone?'"

She started on a third letter. "'Dear Maison, you're the most popular girl in school now and everyone says you're a hero. You know what would make you a hero to me? If you realized I existed. The only person I ever hang out with is my cousin, and he likes to write mean things about people online. You're starting to remind me of him, though. Instead of saying mean things, you treat me like I'm not here, which hurts just as much. Don't you understand?'"

The last paper was stained with a few clear drops of dried water. "Was it raining when you wrote that?" I asked.

"No," Maison said quietly. "Those must be tear-drops."

"There's a reason I picked the online name I did," Destiny said. "My mom used to tell me famous quotes about people's different opinions on destiny, and one said 'destiny is choice, not chance'. Other people have said stuff like that. I thought it was stupid because I never chose to have people bully me and ignore me. A lot of things happen to us because of chance, I think, so I still don't totally agree with the quote. But now I realize it might also mean I can choose what actions I take and my destiny will follow. I choose to help you save the Over-world."

Maison looked her in the eye. "All right," she said. "Go."

CHAPTER 16

WE HAD TO MOVE FAST. I MADE DESTINY A QUICK wooden sword, using two planks of wood and a stick. I knew she needed to have some kind of weapon, just in case, and this was the quickest, easiest sword to make.

It didn't look like zombies would hurt her, but she could run into a skeleton or spider or a creeper. She might even run into TheVampireDragon555 on her way to the portal, and I didn't want to think of that. If she was really on his side, she'd lead him to us. If she ran into him and she wasn't on his side, he'd think she'd betrayed him and who knew what he'd do. I figured she'd be safer running into anything that wasn't TheVampire-Dragon555.

But there was another reason I made her a wooden sword. Wooden swords weren't as strong as a stone sword or a diamond sword. If Destiny did end up betraying us, I didn't want her to have a weapon that could defeat our weapons.

"Thank you, Stevie," Destiny said, taking the wooden sword. "Thank you, Maison. I won't disappoint you."

I opened the door for her and watched until she disappeared in the night.

I turned back to Maison, who was getting us set up to start making potions. "Do you trust her now?"

"I'll trust her when she gets us supplies," Maison said darkly.

I was surprised. "I thought the letters changed your mind," I said.

"Look, I want to trust her, but I don't know if I can," Maison said. "I've seen her at school plenty of times and she seemed harmless. The next thing I know, she's helped someone in a master plan to destroy the whole Overworld. Can you see why I'm a little nervous about her?"

"Yeah," I said in a low voice. "But Ossie likes her."

"Ossie is a cat."

"Ossie is a very smart cat," I corrected.

Ossie started purring again, as if she knew she was being complimented. "See?" I said.

I stood next to Maison at the crafting table and began setting up supplies with her.

"I know our only chance is if she's telling the truth," Maison said. "So we had to let her go. If she's not telling the truth, then our only hope is going to be to go through the portal and save ourselves. If we can't get these potions made, we have nothing else."

I swallowed hard, seeing her point. And then another thought crossed my mind that I hadn't even thought of before. "What if TheVampireDragon555 starts bringing zombies out through the portal into your world?"

It would be like the time at Maison's school, only so much worse because he could keep on making more and more zombies.

Maison shuddered. "That already crossed my mind. I hope . . ." She glanced out the window but all we saw was night. "I hope we can trust her."

Getting busy with the potions gave us something to do.

"Do you think," I said, "if you'd talked to Destiny, none of this would have happened?"

As soon as I said it, I realized I'd said it the wrong way. Offended, Maison said, "Are you trying to say this is my fault?"

"No," I quickly said. Maison had pointed out earlier that even in our wildest dreams we never could have expected this. "I guess it's kind of what Destiny said earlier. She chose to help TheVampireDragon555 and TheVampireDragon555 chose to unleash the zombies. I guess what I'm saying is what we choose to do really can matter."

"Yeah, I noticed her at school," Maison said, hard at work. "She did look pretty miserable and she always kept to herself. Sometimes I wanted to talk to her too, actually." She wiped her hands on her pants. "But I never did."

"Why?" I asked. I was really curious. Maison was so brave.

"Sixth graders don't talk to seventh graders," Maison said.

"Why?" I asked again. That sounded pretty silly to me.

"Because . . . I don't know! I thought if I talked to someone older, it might get me bullied worse. Sometimes the older kids get on the younger kids for even talking to them."

"Do you think Destiny would have gotten on you?" I wondered.

"Her? No," Maison said. "But maybe another seventh or eighth grader would have. They would have seen it as a sixth grader getting 'out of line.'"

"Maybe if you and Destiny talked, you could have banded together and no one would have bugged you," I said. I didn't know if that might work, but I figured it was worth pointing out the possibility.

Maison shook her head, but not like she was disagreeing with me. More like she didn't know what to think. "Talking to a new person is hard sometimes," she said. "What was I supposed to say?"

I thought about it for a moment. "'Hello'?" I suggested.

"Yeah," Maison said softly. She lowered her head over her work. "Yeah," she said again.

"Maybe TheVampireDragon555 is mean because no one ever showed him how to be nice," I said.

"Well, we can talk about all that stuff later," Maison said. "First we just have to stop him from doing anything else."

That's when someone or something began pounding on the roof.

Maison and I both leapt under the table, covering our heads with our arms. *TheVampireDragon555!* I thought. His zombie army was on us.

Maison had been right—Destiny had gone straight back to him and led him to us! She'd played us all for saps!

But when I peered out from under my arms toward the window, I didn't see TheVamprieDragon555 or a zombie army. In the light of the torches, I saw apples and blocks of gold falling from the sky. Some were hitting the roof as they fell. They puddled up by the house, all the supplies we could ever need to make enough potions to save the villagers.

"Stevie?" Maison said.

"Yes, Maison?"

"I think we made the right choice trusting Destiny."

CHAPTER 17

AS SOON AS THE SUPPLIES STOPPED RAINING DOWN, Maison and I raced outside and began collecting them in our arms and taking them inside the house.

By now I had it all figured out how to make the potion and Maison and I worked as quickly as we could. Turn glass into bottles. Pull water from the well Dad had out front. Brew. Add the ingredients.

"We need more water," Maison said.

"I'm on it," I said, heading back out. When I stepped out on the porch, I almost dropped the bucket I was going to collect water in. A zombie was approaching the house, and we didn't have Destiny to keep it at bay! Plus Dad's sword and all the other weapons were in the house.

But then the zombie raised its hand to wave and I realized it was Destiny. The green skin had thrown me off.

"Did it work?" she asked breathlessly as she approached.

"Work!" I exclaimed. "We got tons of stuff! We are all set to make the potions now." I was actually starting to feel hopeful.

Destiny smiled shyly. I didn't think she was used to getting praise and she didn't know how to take it.

As soon as Destiny stepped into the house, Maison jumped on her. Destiny cringed at first as though she expected this to be an attack, and then her dark red eyes opened when she realized Maison was hugging her.

"You did it!" Maison said. "Thank you!"

I didn't know zombies could blush, yet it looked as if Destiny's green cheeks had gotten a little pink in them.

"We don't have much time, though," Destiny said seriously when Maison stepped back. "How are the potions coming along?"

"We're working on them," I said.

Destiny came over and supervised our work. "I don't want to alarm you guys," she began, which instantly got us both alarmed, "but I passed by the village on my way back from the portal. TheVampireDragon555 has rows and rows of zombies lined up. They look like soldiers. I don't think it's going to take him much longer to get all the zombie villagers in order and ready to attack."

This was some heavy duty information to take in. "Did you . . . did you see my dad?" I asked softly. Some part of me was still wishing Dad was strong enough to break the zombie spell on his own.

Destiny hesitated. I could tell she didn't want to tell me. Then she said, "He's in the front line, leading the others."

It took a moment for that to sink in.

"It's only because TheVampireDragon555 is controlling him," Destiny assured me. "We know he wouldn't be like that otherwise."

It didn't matter. That was my dad, who had always gone about doing the right thing and protecting others. Now, with one bite, all that was gone. All thanks to TheVampireDragon555. "You heard Destiny," I said loudly. "Let's hurry."

But I was really just saying it to myself. Maison was already hurrying, and now Destiny joined in, helping us work. I had to tell myself to get to work, because I realized it really was the only option now. I couldn't sit here and worry if TheVampireDragon555 would show up at any minute, or worry about us not stopping him. Or worry that we might have to run through the portal and close off the Overworld forever, because it was the only thing we could do to stop him from destroying more than one world.

I had to make these potions. That's all there was to it.

"Destiny?" Maison said, startling me out of my thoughts.

"Hmm?" Destiny said, fermenting some spider eyes.

"I'm sorry I never spoke to you. I was scared to talk to you, too. I thought the other seventh and eighth graders might get on me. Plus, well, talking to a new person is kind of . . . hard."

Destiny gave her a small smile. "I understand," she said. "It's always been really hard for me to talk to new people. I think that's why I kept hanging out with The-

VampireDragon555, even though I knew he was no good for me. But I let him pull me around."

"You know what else is bugging me?" Maison said. "Why do you keep calling him 'TheVampireDragon555'? You know his real name. Call him that."

Destiny opened her mouth. Closed it. Then opened it again and said, "I call him that because that's all I think of him as anymore. Like I said, he's always been a bully. But somehow once he got to griefing and trolling online, he just got a lot worse. I think it's because it was easier for him to get away with it since he could use a fake name and all that. It's like he became this vampire dragon that just wants to destroy because he thinks it's funny."

She paused again and went on, "This probably sounds crazy, but I also think he doesn't know how much damage he's doing. He wrecks things online and laughs, but he never knows if the person on the other computer is crying or really messed up because of what he's doing."

"I never thought of that," I said. "But he has to see all that he's doing here!" He could look into the eyes of the villagers he turned into zombies. That was way different from typing something in a computer and then walking away.

"I think if he realized the damage he does, he might stop," Destiny said. "I just don't know how to get through to him."

None of us did. Feverishly, we kept working on the potions, desperate to be ready before his zombie army was upon us.

CHAPTER 18

THE POTIONS WERE READY. THE COUNTDOWN WAS now.

"Can I?" Destiny asked timidly, looking over the potions and golden apples. "I want to be human again."

I wondered what that would be like, to be a zombie and know you were one. With the regular zombie villagers, they weren't aware that their skin was green and their eyes were red and they were being controlled. Destiny could look at her skin and feel her body changes and know something was wrong. It had to be really creepy.

"All right," I said. "Let's do this."

I also wanted to make sure the potion would work before we set ourselves up in the tree house. Dad had told me many stories about turning zombie villagers back into villagers, but those stories had all come from before I was born. I had never seen the transformation myself, and I had definitely never made a Potion of Weakness before. Even though Dad had gone over potions with me a million times and I had his book with ingredients, I was still scared we might have done something wrong.

I splashed Destiny with the Potion of Weakness and then gave her a golden apple to eat. That's how Dad and Dad's book said you were supposed to do it.

Thankfully, the change started almost immediately. First little curls of smoke began rising from her body, though I knew that was natural and not something to worry about. Then her body began shaking, and then little red lights began to sizzle around her once she'd gotten the golden apple down. I watched, anxious, hoping.

"How do you feel?" Maison asked.

"I feel funny," Destiny replied. She was still croaking in that dry, zombie voice. A bad sign.

For three minutes Destiny trembled, and those minutes felt as if they might as well have been days. Maison and I watched closely, holding our breaths.

"This seems to be taking a long time," Maison said in distress.

"My dad said it might take a few minutes or so," I said.

"What if it doesn't work?" Maison whispered to me.

I thought back on my lessons with Dad. We were sitting at the table with him grilling me about potions again, and he had said, "Now, Stevie, what happens if the Potion of Weakness and golden apple don't cure a zombie villager?"

"You try again?" I'd said brightly, hoping I was right. I wasn't.

"No," Dad said. "You use your sword."

By that, Dad meant it was all over and all you had left to do was save yourself. So now I said to Maison, "We just hope it works."

"Oh!" Destiny said. "Oh!"

And then the transformation was complete. She was standing there again with her natural brown eyes and body, the red and green all gone.

Maison and I cheered and hugged her.

"I can't believe it." Destiny was gasping and her voice sounded like a normal person's voice again.

"I'm so glad you're better," I said. "Now you won't try to eat your fingers anymore."

"Huh?" Destiny said, confused.

"You tried to eat your fingernails earlier," I reminded her. "I thought it was some zombie thing."

Maison shook her head, but it was like I'd said something funny. "What?" I said, not getting the joke.

"I was biting my nails because I was nervous," Destiny said. "It's a bad habit, not a zombie thing."

"Oh." I looked down at Destiny's hands and my alarm shot up. "Oh, no!" I picked up her one hand. "It didn't work all the way! Your nails still have black splotches on them."

That's when Maison patted me on the back like she was humoring me. "Let's go, Stevie," she said.

"No," I said. "I think we have a real problem here."

"It's nail polish," Maison said dryly.

Destiny looked at her fingernails. "They are kind of chipped."

"Nail polish?" I repeated, at a loss. "Is that some kind of potion?"

"No, it's nothing," Maison said. "We'll explain later." She was hefting up piles of golden apples. "We need to get these to the tree house."

Destiny's nails still looked pretty funny to me, but I dropped it. As we began hauling stuff out the door, I heard a mew.

"Ossie!" I said. She was rubbing against my legs. "We have to take her with us!"

"Why?" Maison asked. "Wouldn't she be safer here?"

"Because . . ." I didn't want to say why. We had good signs on our side: tons of potions and the proof the potion worked on Destiny. Still, that didn't mean we'd be ready for an entire zombie army. If anything happened and we needed to flee, I had to make sure Ossie was with us. We wouldn't have time to run back and get her and then run for the portal.

Both Maison and Destiny got it and they nodded in agreement.

"Come on, Ossie," I said, and the little cat followed us. Maybe she remembered her life before as a wild ocelot and was ready to get out there and take on the world's dangers. Her presence would also protect us from creepers if any tried to get close to us.

I pulled one of Dad's minecarts out of the shed and we filled it with potions and apples. There wasn't enough room for us too, so we pushed it all the way to the tree house. A night wind rustled through, moving Maison and Destiny's hair like silky spiderwebs. My hair stayed in place like a block, but the wind still gave me shivers. I knew it wasn't much longer now.

Ossie climbed up the tree and into the tree house on her own, while Maison, Destiny and I dragged up the supplies. Torches were lit around the tree house, letting us see. When we got all the potions and apples ready, we stood on the balcony. Destiny clutched the wooden sword I'd made her earlier, and Maison had her stone sword. I held Dad's diamond sword tightly.

Please, I thought, holding the diamond sword, *please let me do the right thing and save the Overworld.*

Destiny inhaled a sharp breath and looked out over the horizon. I jumped to alertness, searching for what was out there. I couldn't see anything yet, but my ears could pick up on the sound of many footsteps rumbling the ground. And the sound of hisses and moans. The zombie army was coming, and we could only hope we were ready for them.

CHAPTER 19

THE VAMPIRE DRAGON 555 WAS HAUGHTILY APPROACH-
ing with his army behind him, their feet rumbling
the ground. He'd put some cloth over his shoulders
like a cape, I think to make himself look fancier. There
was also a diamond sword in his hand, one he must have
stolen from the village. The cape swirled out behind him
in a powerful way.

Right at his heels were the rows and rows of zombies.
Some of them were zombie villagers. Some of them were
regular zombies. Many of them were holding weapons
and wore armor.

"All right," I breathed. "This is what we do. When
they get close enough, we start throwing the Potions of
Weakness at the zombie villagers. We need to save them.
The regular zombies were probably made from coding.
We just need to defeat them."

"I'm good at throwing," Maison said. She swung
her arm like a baseball player warming up for practice.
"That's not going to be a problem."

I looked to Destiny. "Do you think you can help me fight the real zombies?"

She gave a long swallow. "I can try."

"Good," I said. "When the zombie villagers turn back, some of them will already have weapons to fight the regular zombies. When we defeat the zombies, if they leave a weapon behind, we need to get those to the weaponless villagers who have changed back."

Destiny nodded. "Right."

Maison, Destiny and I stood very close together, trying to look brave, trying not to show any fear as the rows of zombies continued to draw closer and closer. There were hundreds of them and three of us. Just like Destiny said, Dad was in the front row, right behind TheVampireDragon555.

TheVampireDragon555 stopped before the tree house, waving his cape out behind him. "Destiny!" he crooned in a singsong voice. "Don't tell me you betrayed me!" But it sounded like he found this amusing.

"You're the one who betrayed me!" Destiny shouted, not finding this amusing at all. "You knew I was vulnerable, so you talked me into doing all sorts of crazy things to make you happy. Troll people online. Break into Maison's computer. I'm not going to be your minion anymore. It stops now."

"And you're going to defeat me with that little stick?" TheVampireDragon555 said and laughed, pointing at her sword.

"No," Maison said. "With this."

With a perfect arch of her arm, she hurled a Potion of Weakness at Dad. It hit him dead-center and immediately he began to shake and have curls of gray smoke come out of him. Before TheVampireDragon555 could even figure out what was going on, Maison had thrown a golden apple directly at Dad for him to eat.

"So you've been playing with potions!" TheVampire-Dragon555 said. Before he'd even finished his sentence, Maison, Destiny and I had all thrown more potions and apples out. The zombie villagers were starting to shake and change. But I saw that my first hunch was right: Maison was the best thrower out of the three of us, hitting her mark every time.

"Those potions won't do much!" TheVampireDragon555 crowed. "I can just make more and more zombies!"

"Not without your computer, you can't," Destiny called down. "When I did the codes to make the potion ingredients, I couldn't find a way to stop what you had already done. So I just locked you out of your computer. There's no way you'll find out how to get back in before the sun rises."

"You what?" TheVampireDragon555 thundered. "Why, you good for nothing— "

Ossie jumped up on the balcony and hissed down at him.

With a roar, TheVampireDragon555 came charging to the tree house ladder, diamond sword raised high above his head. He quickly scaled up the ladder.

"We have to stop him!" Destiny exclaimed.

I threw myself partway down the ladder, hitting The-VampireDragon555 with my sword and knocking him back to the ground. By the time he pulled himself to his feet, I'd landed on the ground a few feet from him, sword out.

TheVampireDragon555 wiped his mouth and eyed me. "Father's sword?" He was being snarky.

"Better than the sword you stole," I shot back, and charged him. Our swords clashed.

"Well, aren't you brave," TheVampireDragon555 sneered, bearing his sword down toward me. I realized then that I might have overestimated myself. I was better at sword fighting, I was sure, but TheVampireDragon555 was bigger than me and physically stronger. My feet were digging into the ground as we strained our swords together, trying to knock the other off.

"I'm not someone who uses a computer to attack people," I snapped.

"Of course not." TheVampireDragon555 yanked his sword back. Not expecting this, I stumbled forward and almost fell. "I have a whole army. Zombies, get him!"

I whirled around. A row of zombie villagers were coming at me, moaning, their red eyes standing out in the darkness. But before they could reach me, one, two, three, four, five, six, seven, eight of them got hit with potions, all in order. The zombie villagers stopped and began to shake. Maison threw golden apples down to all of them.

I was about to holler to Maison, "Good timing!" when I heard Destiny cry, "Stevie, look out!"

I turned just in time, barely missing TheVampire-Dragon555's sword. He had used the zombies as a distraction so he could hit me from behind. I felt the whir of the sword against my arm and fell to the ground. The force of the drop momentarily stunned me.

TheVampireDragon555 raised his sword to go after me again. That's when Destiny jumped between us, throwing out her wooden sword to counter TheVampireDragon555's attack. The wooden sword stopped the attack, but the sword splintered. Another hit and it would be broken.

"Get away from him!" Destiny said.

"Risking your safety for someone you barely even know?" TheVampireDragon555 teased. "Why, Destiny, you really will follow anyone rather than think for yourself."

"That's not true," Destiny said, slashing out at him with her sword. He took a step back, dodging her. "Stevie's my friend." She swung again.

This time their swords hit, and Destiny's broke. The force of it knocked her to the ground. TheVampireDragon555 loomed over her, smiling.

"You might have locked me out of my computer," he said. "But I still have the upper hand here. I can do a lot of damage before the sun rises."

Destiny kicked him in the shin and he hopped back in pain, favoring his leg. "That's where you're wrong," she said, rising. "We won't let you. You've done enough damage."

When he came after her again, I was up on my feet and ready. I slammed into TheVampireDragon555, knocking him back.

"The villagers are starting to change!" I heard Maison shout from overhead. "Villagers!" she called to them.

"You've been turned into zombies and that tall zombie with a cape is the one who did it. Turn the other villagers back! Stop the real zombies! Get their weapons! The sun will rise soon."

I couldn't look over my shoulder at what was happening, but TheVampireDragon555 took a look and his green face filled with rage. He hit me hard with his sword, knocking me down again. But instead of attacking me, he ran into the middle of the zombie army, ordering, "Zombies! Zombies, obey me! Get anyone who isn't a zombie! GET THEM!"

"Stevie!" Dad said, running to my side. He helped me get back on my feet. "My sword," he said in confusion, seeing it in my hand. "What is going on?"

The red eyes were gone. The green skin had turned to its normal brown color. His eyes were his eyes again, looking at me with wild concern.

"It's just what Maison said," I replied. "We have to turn the villagers back and stop the zombies. The zombie with the cape is the one who started it all."

Behind us was chaos. Zombies were charging toward the newly-changed villagers. Maison was hitting more and more villagers with potions and apples. She'd gotten almost all of them. And villagers were seizing up weapons that zombies had dropped, and were going into battle mode.

I couldn't see TheVampireDragon555 in the horde, though I could still hear him screaming, calling orders out to the army of zombies.

"We need to stop him," I said, rushing toward the crowd.

"Stevie, wait!" Dad called, but he was right behind me, picking up a sword he found on the ground.

I pushed my way through the villagers. A real zombie reared up in front of me to block my way. I slashed the diamond sword through it, making it disappear immediately.

"Where are you, you vampire dragon?" I yelled. "Stop hiding behind the zombies like you hide behind a computer screen!"

From out of the zombie swarm I heard him yell, "Get him! Get the one called Stevie!"

Maybe he thought once he'd taken me out, it'd be clear sailing for him. But his plan backfired. All the zombies tried to circle around me, and this made the whole scene less confusing because they were all heading in the same direction now. Dad and the other villagers circled around me too, each hitting the zombies one by one before they could get to me.

Now most of the zombies in the army were taken out.

TheVampireDragon555 must have noticed this, because suddenly he shouted, "Clear off! Clear off!"

"Stevie, I see him!" Maison hollered from the tree house, pointing. "He's over there."

I broke through the circle of villagers, running in the direction she pointed. TheVampireDragon555 was just ahead, only a handful of zombies at his heels. They were all regular zombies now, no zombie villagers. Destiny was in front of me, going at him with a new wooden sword.

"Put that down, Destiny!" he said. "I won't hurt you if I don't have to."

"Liar!" Destiny shot back. "You're just a coward and you know you've lost!"

Her words inflamed him even more. He swung his sword back to hit her, but he made a terrible mistake. His sword knocked into a zombie next to him. He didn't hit the zombie hard enough to make it disappear, though he hit it hard enough to make it angry. As soon as the first zombie got angry, the others did, too, like a chain reaction. They were all hissing and roaring. Sometimes when one mob attacks another, it throws them off and they attack their own kind.

And just like that, all the remaining zombies turned on TheVampireDragon555, ready to destroy him.

CHAPTER 20

"NO!" THEVAMPIREDRAGON555 SCREAMED. IN HIS panic, he slashed out furiously toward the zombies, with no sense of what he was doing. He made one zombie disappear, but only enraged the others more. They dove on top of their prey.

"Don't let the zombies get him!" I said to Dad and the others fighting. I wanted TheVampireDragon555 stopped, not destroyed. I flung myself into the group of zombies, hitting them with my sword. One zombie turned away from TheVampireDragon555 and came at me. With one sharp slash I took care of it. Destiny was hitting the zombies, too, and then there was Dad, taking out two with one hit.

"No! No! Help!" TheVampireDragon555 was crying under the pile. Somehow he'd dropped his sword and he had his hands up over his face, trying to protect himself.

"Look!" Destiny said.

A sliver of light appeared over the horizon.

The zombies hissed and jumped back. They hated the light.

As the sun rose, their bodies began to smoke, and then to flame. The last of them burst into fire and vanished.

Soon only theVampireDragon555 lay there on the ground, unharmed and panting. If the zombies had bitten him, it obviously didn't have an effect, since, after all, he already was a zombie. But the fact that he wasn't from the Overworld had also given him another advantage, since he hadn't burned like all the other zombies.

He started to sit up but found he couldn't get far. Destiny, Dad and I all had our swords at the ready, pointing at him so he knew not to go anywhere.

TheVampireDragon555 looked at the swords, looked at our stony faces, and then looked at the buttery, soft light going all over the land. Slowly he raised his green hands in surrender.

The villagers were standing behind us, and they cleared a path to let Maison walk through. In one hand she held a Potion of Weakness and in the other, a golden apple.

"Jig's up, VampireDragon555," she said, stopping in front of him.

"You saved my life," TheVampireDragon555 said to me, stunned. "You could have let the zombies get me."

I never thought red eyes could look so bittersweet and sad, but his did. He really expected me to let the zombies get him.

"I'm not like you," I said. "If I fight, it's to protect myself and others in self-defense. I would never hurt another living thing for *fun*."

He gave a long swallow, watching me. "But," he stuttered, "I still don't understand. If I were you, I wouldn't have saved my enemy when he was down. Why did you do that?"

"Because," I said softly, "it was the right thing to do."

"Where are you from, stranger?" Dad demanded. "You're not from this world, and I can tell you this: you're *not* welcome back in this world."

"We're from the same world Maison is from," Destiny said.

The villagers all turned their eyes on her. She looked a little embarrassed and quickly continued, "I am so sorry for all this. We hacked into Maison's account and used it to create our own portal here. I never knew any of this would happen, so I joined with Stevie and Maison to stop it. With your help, I want you to join me in destroying the portal we made so we can't get through again. This is your world, not ours."

"You know this zombie?" Dad asked her, gesturing toward TheVampireDragon555.

"Yes," Destiny said. "He's my cousin, Yancy."

"Yancy?" I repeated. "You just tried to destroy an entire world and your name is *Yancy*?"

TheVampireDragon555, er, Yancy, looked down as though ashamed. "Yeah," he muttered.

"Well, Yancy," Dad said in his no-nonsense voice. "Why did you attack the Overworld and do such terrible things to the villagers?"

Yancy didn't look so big and scary now. And, like any normal person, he was intimidated by Dad. "Because," he said weakly, "it's the only thing that makes me feel good about myself. It's the only thing I can do."

"That's how I used to feel, too." Destiny threw her sword on the ground. "But I'm tired of acting that way."

"I never knew there were people like you out there," Yancy said, looking at me, and then at Maison. "You risked your lives to help the villagers. Most of them were people you didn't even know. You could have just gotten out of the portal and never looked back. You even risked your lives for *me*."

He looked down at his green hands. "This will give me a lot to think about. I thought stuff about heroes was just from books. But you two are heroes."

Dad put his hand on Destiny's shoulder. "I think she's a hero as well. I saw her fighting to save us, too."

Destiny smiled shyly. "Thank you, sir."

"And Stevie," Dad said. "I shouldn't have been so hard on you about memorizing potions. I see you've mastered them just fine."

"Well . . ." I said, a little shy. "I probably should study them a *bit* more."

"All right, Yancy," Maison said. "It's time to go." She splashed him with the Potion of Weakness and handed him the apple, watching as he transformed back into a human being.

CHAPTER 21

A WEEK LATER, MAISON AND I WERE BUSY BREWING in Dad's house. We were working on the Potion of Swiftness. Dad said he saw my point that it was easier to learn potions by making them instead of just memorizing them. To make a Potion of Swiftness, you needed glass bottles filled with water, Nether Wart and some sugar.

It wasn't just about potions, though. I also wanted Maison to fill me in on everything that had happened in her world since we'd last seen each other.

"You want to know the craziest thing?" she said. "I got home thinking my mom would kill me for being gone for so long. But I'd only been gone twenty minutes. She thought I was just doing my homework or playing *Minecraft* in my room. Yancy must have done something with codes to change the time while he was in there. It's a mystery."

"But what about . . .?" She knew what I really wanted to know. After Yancy had turned back into a human, we'd all gone to the portal they'd created and sent both him and Destiny back. And then Maison, Dad and I had destroyed the portal so they couldn't return. Maison's and my portal, which was protected by a specially-built house, was still around for the two of us to use.

"Well, the first thing I did was get a firewall so no one can hack my computer again," Maison said. "My mom was confused when I ran downstairs saying I needed a firewall ASAP. But then I showed her the stuff Yancy had been writing about me online and said I'd feel safer if I had a firewall."

"What did your mom say?"

"She said she was proud of me for telling her about the cyberbullying. She said you shouldn't ignore it when it gets serious like that. You should tell an adult. I told her that I knew Yancy's real identity, so she called his mom. It turns out Yancy was talking to his mom right then with Destiny there, admitting that he'd been trolling people for years and he needed help. His mom has him seeing a therapist for his anger issues. One of the things his therapist had him do was write an apology letter to me. In the letter, he said, 'I will never go to the Overworld again. You have my word.' The therapist and his parents didn't get that, but I did."

"What about Destiny?" I asked.

"We don't have any classes together," Maison said. "But we hang out at lunch every day now. She doesn't bite her nails so much anymore."

"Are her nails still splotchy?" I asked. "Are you sure that's not a zombie sign?"

Maison sighed. "I'm sure."

Ossie came up, purring, rubbing against both Maison and me. The Potion of Swiftness was just about ready and Dad came over to check it.

"Looks good," he said with pride. "I have two very talented potion makers here. The next time you have to save everyone, you'll be ready."

"Next time?" I echoed hesitantly.

"Well, sure," Dad said. "I'm a farmer and a miner, and that's what I always thought you'd be someday, Stevie. But the more I think about it, I think you and Maison are going to grow up to be heroes."

"Aww, Dad," I said, embarrassed. But I could tell from Maison's smile she liked the compliment.

"That's not a word I throw around lightly," Dad said. "However, both of you did save Maison's school, and then you saved the Overworld. I think someday the Overworld will be telling stories about the adventures of Stevie and Maison."

"Or the adventures of Maison and Stevie," Maison corrected.

"I know the perfect way to figure out whose name should come first," I joked. "We'll both take the Potion of Swiftness, and whoever reaches the tree house first wins."

"You're on," Maison exclaimed.

We each doused ourselves with the potion. And then we took off running across the field at super speed, laughing as the sunlight poured down on us and our tree house came into view.